We come in peace . . .

The Martian Ambassador's teeth clicked and chattered. The translator droned: "We come in peace. We come in peace. We come in peace."

The crowd was delighted. Applause rippled and swelled. A happy hippie released a white dove. People laughed and cheered, and applauded all the louder when the dove fluttered over the Martian Ambassador.

The Martian rolled his great red eyes, lifted an odd device, and *blasted the bird to oblivion*! Before its charred feathers could hit the ground, the Martians leveled their ray guns at the crowd . . .

A novelization by Ron Fontes and Justine Korman
Screen story and screenplay by Jonathan Gems
Based upon MARS ATTACKS,
a property of the Topps Company

Copyright © 1996 Warner Bros.
Based on MARS ATTACKS®, the copyrighted property
of the Topps Company, Inc.

Photos © 1996 Warner Bros.
Photos by Bruce W. Talamon and Industrial Light and Magic.

Published by Troll Communications L.L.C.

Printed in the United States of America.

10 9 8 7 6 5 4 3 2 1

Tuesday, May 9—6:57 P.M.
Four miles outside of Lockjaw, Kentucky

The rolling green hills of Kentucky were bathed in the golden glow of a southern sunset. A gentle breeze rustled the bluegrass on the lawn of an old gray farmhouse.

The side door banged open as Mr. Lee carried a garbage bag outside. Mr. Lee strolled to the garbage can beside the road. He took a deep breath of the fresh country air and savored the smell of burning leaves. His struggle to come to this country from the Philippines had been worth it. Lee worked very hard in the big city to afford a little farm where he could grow vegetables and raise his children in peace.

Mr. Lee saw his neighbor chugging up the hill on a rusty tractor. Lee had always thought of Mr. Grant as "the hillbilly" because of his long, skinny frame and long, scrawny beard, not to mention his silly hat. He looked like a cartoon character. But Mr. Lee kept these thoughts to himself because he was a polite man. Besides, Mr. Grant had never done him any harm, and, for all he knew, Mr. Lee might look a bit funny to Mr. Grant.

"Howdy, Mr. Lee." Mr. Grant waved a long,

skinny arm. "What is this, the Filipino New Year's?"

Mr. Lee was puzzled. "No. Why do you say that?"

"Smells like y'all are cookin' up a feast. A body can smell it clear over from the Interstate. What is it, a barbecue?" his neighbor asked.

Mr. Lee sniffed the air. The enticing odor *did* smell like meat. No one burns leaves in May. There was more: a sound, like artillery, or thunder . . . and screaming!

"What's that noise?" Mr. Grant shouted as the ground shook and a dull roar filled their ears.

Mrs. Lee and two screaming children ran from the house with the dog barking at their heels.

"Oh, my Lord!" cried Mr. Grant.

Mr. Lee turned just in time to see a herd of cows stampede across his garden from behind the house. Flames leaped from their bounding bodies.

The Lees pushed their children atop the tractor and scrambled to join them as the burning bovines rumbled around them. Above the sounds of the sobbing children and the cries of the doomed beasts, Mr. Lee heard an eerie, throbbing hum. He looked up to see a silvery disk in the sky.

Mr. Lee was the first to realize that no place on Earth is safe when . . .

Wednesday, May 10—11:25 A.M.
Washington, D.C.

James Dale, President of the United States, was shaken to the core by what he had just seen: photos from the Hubble Space Telescope. The first picture showed large disks rising out of craters on a rocky red planet. Dale was informed that it was the planet Mars, named for the Roman god of war.

The next few photos clearly depicted a fleet of flying disks approaching Earth. These objects were crossing 35 million miles in a matter of hours!

This was no hoax. Real flying saucers! How could he milk this to the max? And most of all—what would it mean for the next election?

Dale looked around the Oval Office, trying to assess the mood of the men surrounding him. There was the British professor, Donald Kessler. The President could read nothing off Kessler's cool, know-it-all exterior.

General Decker paced and strutted like a bloodthirsty hawk eager to fly into battle. The President knew that Decker would want to fight whatever was in those saucers no matter what happened. But how would the voters feel?

Dale looked to General Casey for the reasonable approach. Casey's warm brown eyes and round face spoke of his humane, diplomatic attitude. But the wimpy, sensible approach might not be popular either.

The only safe person to ask was his press secretary, Jerry Ross. Ross's long nose, tiny eyes, and fawning manner reminded the President of a smelly, overeager puppy, but Jerry knew the public. Dale asked, "What's your take on this, Jerry?"

"The people are gonna love it!" Jerry practically drooled. "Our only decision is whether to ambush the six o'clock news or hold out for prime time."

Decker screeched, "No press! This situation is on a need-to-know. We've got to keep this top secret and go immediately to DefCon Four."

"Mr. President," Jerry whined. "We can't sit on this!"

The President ignored him. "General Casey, what's your opinion?"

Casey didn't want to commit to anything

unless he absolutely had to. "Well, sir. Do we know they're hostile?" he asked thoughtfully.

"They've got thousands of warships circling the planet!" General Decker squawked.

"Do we know they're warships?" Casey wondered in a mellow, fatherly tone.

"Professor, what do we know about them?" Dale asked.

Kessler replied, "We know they're highly advanced technologically, which suggests very strongly that they're peaceful. An advanced civilization is by definition not barbaric. This is a great day, Mr. President. I and all my colleagues are extremely excited."

Decker was very excited too. But Dale ignored the general's sputtered objections.

Kessler had told the President just what he wanted to hear. Dale already knew he would wear his blue Cerruti suit to deliver what would be the speech of a lifetime. He said, "Jerry, I'll need a good speech, statesmanlike, historical, but warm and neighborly. Abraham Lincoln meets *Leave it to Beaver*—you know the kind of thing."

Jerry knew just what the President meant.

★

While President James Dale prepared himself for his place in history, First Lady Marsha Dale planned to revise some history of her own. Marsha's revisions required the help of a decorator, an upholsterer, and lots of tax dollars. She wanted to redecorate the whole White House. She was an elegant woman with frosty blonde hair and a well-tailored red suit. Her makeup and nails were immaculate. Her shoes were of the finest Italian leather.

Marsha's teenage daughter, Taffy, dressed quite differently. Her long, straight hair was tangled. She walked around the White House barefoot, in baggy jeans and a drab plaid shirt over a Nirvana T-shirt.

Taffy watched her mother skeptically and said, "Why don't you leave the Roosevelt Room the way the Roosevelts wanted it?"

"Because Eleanor Roosevelt was too fond of chintz," the First Lady scolded.

Taffy was exasperated. "Mother, this is not your house!"

★ ★ ★ ★

Wednesday, May 10—4:30 P.M.
Las Vegas, Nevada

Byron Williams was used to flashing cameras. But the ex-champ wasn't in the ring now. He was posing for a picture with three nuns.

Byron regretted that he had never thought ahead much. He'd always been as strong as a bull. There was only one thing he had wanted to do with his tremendous strength: He'd wanted to be a fighter. Byron pursued that dream with a single-minded devotion that had made him the heavyweight champion of the world!

But then he got old. Byron hadn't planned on that. As his reflexes slowed and his eyes got blurry, he couldn't fight in the ring. Byron had to start looking around for money. He had a family to support.

Byron got mixed up in some ugly stuff. He did bad things with bad people. And he paid the greatest price: losing the woman he loved and their two sons.

After his brush with the law, Byron was put out to pasture. Now, with his mighty form draped in a glitzy gladiator costume, Byron was the official greeter for the Luxor Hotel and Casino.

The giant building was coated with an electric dazzle of lights, neon, and mirrors. Inside were vast rooms full of little old ladies tirelessly pulling levers on slot machines. The huge, ritzy casino was fogged with smoke and buzzing with voices. Music leaked out of showrooms, where guests saw more glitz and glamour, showgirls, and big acts like Tom Jones.

Sooner or later everyone came to Vegas, even some nuns. The sisters fondly recalled Byron's boxing career. But their reverie was interrupted by a loudspeaker paging Byron to the telephone.

As he crossed the crowded casino, everyone from Cindy, the pretty waitress, to Art Land, the big-wheel real-estate developer, greeted the friendly boxer.

Just as he was an ex-champ, Byron was also an ex-husband. The voice at the other end of the phone belonged to Louise, the love of Byron's life. He knew this was bound to be trouble. Louise never called him at work.

Mr. Bava, the casino manager, glared at Byron, which meant more trouble later. Bava was strict. Byron wanted to stay on the manager's good side.

Louise spoke in a tense whisper, which meant she was calling from her job at the Washington D.C. Telephone Exchange. "The boys have been gone for two days."

Byron felt the words like a blow to the gut. This was the worst kind of trouble. Their teenage sons, Cedric and Neville, had been skipping school. Now they'd spent two nights away from home! Louise didn't say it, but Byron knew what she was thinking. They might be out with a gang, and that meant guns and other kinds of trouble.

And Byron was right. At that very moment, the boys were shooting tin cans in a condemned building.

No wonder Louise was frantic. But what could Byron do? You couldn't punch your way out of this kind of trouble.

"Let me come back," Byron blurted. "I've changed."

Louise said, "A leopard doesn't change its spots."

"This one has," Byron said sincerely. In the depths of his lonely despair, he had found God.

Louise sighed. "I wish I could believe it."

Byron glanced at the angry manager. "Are you

still cool with me coming to Washington?" he asked quickly.

Louise said, "Yeah. Take care, honey. Bye."

Byron wished he was going straight to Washington. But instead, he trudged back to work. His heart was heavy with trouble. All around him other troubled people drowned themselves in watered drinks and the empty hope of easy riches.

In a nearby bar booth, Art Land and his wife, Barbara, bickered. Barbara had recently discovered ecology, crystals, herbs, and all things New Age. She struggled to enlighten her greedy, crooked husband, Art.

She didn't get it. Art used to be an okay guy. Now he was a rich rat. The more money he had, the less okay he was.

For his part, Art wondered why Barbara was always nagging him. Why couldn't she understand that you had to be crooked to do business in Vegas? Couldn't she see that his Galaxy Hotel would be the biggest casino ever? It was the wave of the future, a world-class hotel with 10,000 rooms, a $5 million space ride, a restaurant shaped like a flying saucer, and a whole building full of virtual reality!

"But don't you realize what you're doing?" Barbara fussed. "You're destroying the Earth. All this greed, this money system, we're destroying everything!"

"I'm sick of hearing your New Age bunk," Art growled. Here he was on the brink of real success, and she wanted him to hug a whale. Art just wanted his shot at the big time. It wasn't like it was the end of the world.

* ★ * ★

Wednesday, May 10—7:50 P.M.
New York City

As dusk fell over the teeming streets and mighty skyscrapers of Manhattan, Jason Stone admired himself on a monitor at the GNN studios. *Hair's good. I like the hair,* he thought as his video image reported the latest news from the United Nations.

The mellow sound of Jason's voice purred over the excellent sound system in his perfect office. Jason was proud of the calm dignity of this most professional newsroom. GNN was the hub of the world, and he was at the hub of the hub! Jason knew everything as soon as it happened. It didn't get any better than this.

The phone rang. Jason flipped it open and brushed his hair carefully aside. He heard the voice of his gorgeous girlfriend, Nathalie West. The chaos and confusion of her madcap *Today in Fashion* newsroom almost drowned out her words.

Jason pictured Nathalie's little Chihuahua, Poppy, scrambling around on her sloppy desk. Nathalie was cool, cute, and very perky, sort of a *That Girl* for the '90s. Her hair looked great on camera. Jason couldn't understand why she would work for a glorified radio station when she could be working for GNN.

Nathalie screamed, "This is big! President Dale is cutting in on 'Unplugged'!"

"That's absurd," Jason scoffed. "Why would he stoop to being on *Today in Fashion*?"

"He's interrupting *everybody*!" Nathalie exclaimed. "They're making an emergency announcement."

Jason was stunned. "You heard before us?"

Just then, a door slammed open. Jason's boss shrieked, "Everyone get to a monitor! The White House is going out *live!*"

Every eye in the studio was riveted on TV screens glowing with the bright blue presidential seal. The eagle spread its wings on every screen in the nation. Every channel. Everywhere. People knew something very important was happening.

The American eagle gave way to President Dale in his blue Cerruti suit. He sat in a comfortable leather armchair before a roaring fire. A bust of Lincoln occupied the mantle, and a portrait of George Washington hung on the wall. The President's golden retriever, Rusty, lay at his master's feet.

The President smiled and apologized for interrupting the regular programming. Then he gave the speech.

This was the most important speech in history. Every newshound in the nation was sure of it, although for the wrong reasons. President James Dale knew it too. Again, for the wrong reasons. But James Dale was making the most of the moment. He took his time.

The usually cool reporters at GNN scrambled

to guess what the President was saying.

Jason yelled, "He's freed the hostages!"

Someone else shouted, "He's not running for reelection," and one lonely optimist cried, "They've balanced the budget!"

Dale droned on, "How many of us know with absolute certainty that history is in the making? How many know the day? How many know the hour?"

In a sloppy little corner of the White House, surrounded by posters of famous suicides, Taffy clutched her teddy bear. She stuffed another handful of Cheetos in her mouth and groaned, "Get to the point."

* ★ * ★

Wednesday, May 10—7:15 P.M.
Perkinsville, Kansas

Richie Norris also wished the President would come to the point. He was watching a tiny portable tube on the counter in the Perkinsville donut shop. Flanked by racks of raw donuts on their dull metal trays, Richie tried to make sense out of President Dale's really long speech.

Rosie the waitress looked bored as ever. She wiped the counter with the slow indifference of a robot whose batteries were running down. *Totally zoned*, Richie thought.

The only customer was this homeless dude nursing a cold cup of coffee and reading a newspaper. Like who bothered with newspapers in Perkinsville? Nothing ever happened in Perkinsville.

Richie and the donut shop were in the kind of town that people drove through on their way to somewhere else. It was an intersection with a gas station, a bus stop, and a mini-mall, and in the mini-mall was the dusty donut shop.

And in the dusty donut shop, Richie tried to figure out what the President was talking about. It was something big and awesome, he had made that much clear, and then he said something about the Hubble Space Telescope and computers and the dawn of a new era. And then there were pictures of . . .

★ ★ ★ ★

New York

". . . a large fleet of vehicles that can best be described as flying saucers. These flying saucers have emerged from the planet Mars and at their current course and speed will be entering Earth's orbit in approximately sixteen hours." With that, the President paused.

When the pictures appeared on-screen, the GNN and *Today in Fashion* studios responded exactly alike. People screamed and yelled and ran around trying to find a way to cover the story.

Jason pushed hair out of his eyes and rallied his troops. He wanted NASA and man-in-the-street reactions. He wanted Carl Sagan!

Nathalie was also screaming. But she just wanted to make sure the Martians came on after Michael Jackson.

★ ★ ★

Las Vegas, Nevada

No one was playing the machines at the Luxor. The big room was eerily quiet, except for the fatherly drone of the President's voice. And then the pictures flashed on the screens. Gigantic spaceships from another world! A whole fleet! And it wasn't a movie!

Cindy gasped. Byron's jaw dropped. This was beyond belief. What were the little troubles of his life beside this?

Across town, Barbara Land lit another candle in her lavish home. Her eyes shone with excitement. Everything she'd learned in her New Age classes pointed to this great moment. The advanced creatures from space were coming like angels to save humanity from its own destructive greed.

She raised her arms to the chandelier and prayed: "Martians! This is great! Please come to Earth, please! We need you!"

Her husband, Art, needed a deal. He needed more money, more time, and more investors for his grand scheme. The more he had, the more he needed. Most of all, he needed to work the phones before the East Coast shut down for the night. And nobody was paying attention. They were all watching some garbage on the tube.

While the President yakked about the twentieth century being a time of borders falling and friendship extending, and the world becoming one planet, Art hunched over the phone in his ritzy office in his unfinished hotel. Only the main tower and the flying saucer restaurant stood above a giant foundation. The rest of Art's grand scheme was under construction.

Art was so busy building a foundation of lies, he didn't hear the President say, "It is profoundly moving to know that there is intelligent life out there."

★ ★ ★

Washington, D.C.

And the President didn't hear Taffy say, "Glad they've got it somewhere." She hugged her teddy bear and looked up at all her posters of rock 'n' roll suicides. How could her father be such a dork? Who was he trying to be this time, Abraham Lincoln? He made all these speeches, and he never meant any of them. Taffy swore she would never be like that.

She glared at the TV as her father concluded solemnly, "Our lives and our world will never be quite the same again."

For once in his long political career, James Dale spoke the perfect truth.

* ★ * ★

Thursday, May 11—6:02 A.M.
New York City

Excited as people were about the Martians, life went on. The next morning started off like any other. People got up. They had breakfast. They read the papers. So did Jason Stone and Nathalie West. She loved a sitcom breakfast. It was so Ward and June.

"EXISTENCE OF INTERPLANETARY LIFE CONFIRMED," said the headline of the good, gray *New York Times*. Jason peered over its inky folds and said, "This is intense!" He was having a great hair day, and the biggest story of the century was breaking. Life didn't get better than this.

Nathalie looked back across the breakfast table. She was crunching cereal and perusing the *New York Post*, which proclaimed, "MARTIANS!!!!" This whole thing was like an episode of *Mystery Science Theatre*.

The phone rang. Jason was disappointed to learn the call was for Nathalie. He was even more upset when she told him that *Today in Fashion* had booked an interview with the President's science advisor.

"Donald Kessler?" Jason squeaked. He couldn't believe it. What was the world coming to when *Today in Fashion* beat out GNN?

Nathalie smirked. "I can't help it if your people are too slow." She cooed to her little dog, "Isn't that right, Poppy?"

Jason sulked and went back to his newspaper. He flipped to the real estate section and saw a great investment opportunity in Las Vegas: Art Land's Galaxy Hotel.

★ ★ ★

Thursday, May 11—9:37 A.M.
Perkinsville, Kansas

"KENTUCKY FRIED CATTLE!" screamed the headline on the *Weekly World News*. The newspaper was clutched in the chubby fingers of Richie's mom, Sue-Ann Norris.

Sue-Ann was a heavy woman stuffed in a cheap slip. Her head was adorned with curlers. She moved her lips as she read the shocking account of the Lee family of Kentucky.

Richie squeezed past her to leave their crowded trailer. He thought the photo was far-out!

Outside, morning sunlight glinted off the piles of junk in the yard. The Norris family's shabby trailer shared the weeds with an assortment of hopeless appliances and rusty car parts. The old, dusty red pickup truck seemed like just another heap of junk.

The Norrises were good, old-fashioned Americans. They worked hard, paid their taxes, and reserved the right to gripe about it. They were the salt of the earth.

Richie could hear his family inside. Billy-Glenn was showing off again for their dad, Big

Glenn. Richie's older brother was blindfolded and scrambling to put together his army rifle. Billy-Glenn was good at stuff like that. Richie never was. His big brother was kind of a meathead, but he was all right.

"Finished!" Billy-Glenn yelled.

Dad clicked the stopwatch in his rough, farmer's hand. "One minute, fifty-seven seconds," he reported with pride.

Billy-Glenn laughed. "I told you. Under two minutes!"

"You did, son," Dad agreed. Richie knew Dad was proud of Billy-Glenn's army career. He hoped someday Dad would be proud of him too.

Richie tugged the handle of an industrial-size refrigerator just outside the trailer door. He took out a box of donuts. Richie heard the TV as he came back inside and offered donuts to his family.

"How old are they?" Sue-Ann asked.

"Fresh baked Friday," Richie replied.

"Richie, that's six days ago," Sue-Ann scoffed. "Okay, gimme two."

The box was passed around. Everyone took a donut, and Richie made sure Grandma got one. She was eighty-eight years old and totally senile.

Most of the family ignored her, but she was all right, as long as she could have her Slim Whitman records. Richie figured Slim was sort of like the Grateful Dead to her or something. Anyway, he loved his grandma.

"This Martian thing is awesome, huh?" Richie ventured.

Grandma gummed a donut. "Has anyone seen my Muffy?"

"Your brother's gonna volunteer," Glenn told Richie with manly pride.

"Soon as I get back to the base," Billy-Glenn bragged around a mouthful of donut. He brushed crumbs off the uniform hanging behind him.

"Volunteer for what?" Richie asked.

"Martian detail." Billy-Glenn stood a bit taller.

Richie grinned. "Cool."

Dad got red in the face. "I tell ya, if any of them Martians come around here, I'm gonna kick their butts!"

★ ★ ★ ★

Washington, D.C.

General Decker was having the very same thought. The Martians were at the top of his list, of course, but it was a long list. And Jerry Ross was next up for a close encounter with Decker's boot.

That press secretary weasel was always turning the President against Decker's plans. Now the little creep was probably cruising around in his limo, acting like a big shot to impress a pair of floozies. Guys like him didn't deserve the power they had.

You wouldn't find General Decker partying. No, sir! Decker had a respectable leisure-time activity: golf. Fresh air, exercise. A good, clean sport, played on a smooth, green, exclusive Georgetown golf course.

The general was currently winning against three lower-ranking officers. Their games were a bit off because they were all grumbling about the President's Martian policy.

"So what did the President say?" one officer asked.

Decker mocked, "He said 'peace and love.'

Open the doors and let the invaders in."

"George Bush would never have let this happen," a major commented. They all grunted.

Decker looked thoughtful. He was fiercely loyal to his country and President. He'd spent his whole life defending America's freedom. He had a warrior's instincts. Alarm bells were going off in his head, even if the softies refused to face reality.

Decker clutched his golf club and looked suspiciously at the caddies. He lowered his voice and led the officers a short distance away. "Look, without going through official channels, I want to put the reserves on alert. What do you say? Let's beef up the troops, just in case."

They all grunted.

★

In downtown Washington, D.C., Cedric and Neville Williams had almost made it out the door when they were stopped by a harsh voice. "Hey, where are you going? Come back here. I want to talk to you."

The boys froze in their tracks. It was their mother, Louise, acting like a cop. "Do you think it's smart to cut school?"

"No, Mama," the boys said with careful calm.

But that was exactly what they had done. Mama wouldn't understand, but Byron's sons knew they lived in a dangerous world. They were teaching themselves the skills they'd need in their own private survival course.

They'd learned a lot yesterday. They'd practiced economics in a couple of alleys, then exercised their geography navigating around town. The city was its own kind of jungle, and even Tarzan carried a knife.

Louise echoed, "'No, Mama,'—'cause it's dumb. You're gonna flunk. You're gonna get in trouble. You're gonna go to jail. You foolin' with guns?"

"No, Mama." But just yesterday afternoon the boys had debated the finer points of a Glock versus a police special. Then they had refined their marksmanship on tin cans until they went home to Officer Louise.

"You messin' with drugs?"

"No, Mama." Drugs would spoil their aim.

Louise knew the boys were lying about something. Though she wouldn't admit it, she really hoped that when Byron got here he'd straighten them out.

★ ★ ★

Las Vegas, Nevada

Byron Williams had finally worked up the courage to take the bull by the horns and ask his manager for a raise. Byron hated this talk stuff. For him, it was never a fair fight. But he needed the money for Louise and the boys, just like when he was back in the ring.

So Byron pretended he heard the bell and set off across the floor of the Luxor. Cindy was serving the Martian Special cocktail and dealing with rude customers. The pretty waitress gave Byron an encouraging smile.

Byron stood up straight and said, "Mr. Bava, can we speak in private?"

From that point on, every answer was a punch. No, the manager had to watch the floor. He couldn't give Byron a raise. He didn't care that times were hard and Byron was supporting a family.

Bava jabbed at Byron's divorce. And in a final flurry of low blows, the manager said, "I can get Leon Spinks or Buster Douglas for the same money, okay? Maybe less." He looked at his watch. "Get moving. You're on in five minutes."

Byron went back to his corner, a champ no more. He was down for the count.

★ ★ ★

New York City

"5 . . . 4 . . . 3 . . . 2 . . . 1 . . ." A *Today in Fashion* assistant director counted down to the end of the first commercial break. Dr. Donald Kessler and Nathalie West had made good use of their off-air time. They were now on a first-name basis.

The two celebrities sat close together on a small, jazzy set. Makeup people fluttered around them. The director paced the floor, babbling about great ratings. Nathalie and Donald were already giving each other rave reviews. It was admiration at first sight.

Nathalie was entranced by the dark-haired scientist's bright blue eyes and heroic jaw. Kessler glanced out of the corner of his eye. Nathalie's golden curls and radiant smile made her the most heavenly body he'd ever seen.

Jason Stone didn't have to be there to know what was going on. Nathalie used to smile at him that way, back when things were right and GNN got the big stories before *Today in Fashion*.

Jason watched Nathalie's interview with the chairman of the American Academy of Astronautics. He hoped she'd mess up or say something dumb. Instead, Jason seemed to be watching a love story! What did Nathalie see in that egghead? His hair was terrible!

Nathalie simpered, "Professor, isn't it weird that we sent a space probe to Mars and didn't even find anyone?"

"Not really, uh, Nathalie." Kessler practically blushed as he said her name. "You see, we didn't go into the canals. The Martian canals are actually canyons, some of them over a hundred miles deep. Martian civilization has clearly developed under the planet's surface." The scientist smiled enthusiastically. "Their science and technology must be mind-boggling! They have a lot to teach us."

"Why haven't we seen evidence of Martians before?" Nathalie wondered.

"I'm positive we have," Kessler declared.

Nathalie was intrigued. "You mean, UFOs?"

Kessler nodded, and Nathalie continued her questions. "So what in your view are some of the things the Martians can teach us, professor?"

"Quite a lot about Mars, I expect." The scientist chuckled; Nathalie joined in. They exchanged sparkling glances.

Jason gasped. "She's flirting with him!"

A nearby reporter shrugged. Jason spluttered while Kessler nattered on about beautiful visions of a wonderful future with the Martians. And then the TV picture distorted, and flashed, and went off.

"Aw, now what?" Jason whined.

"Maybe it's the cable?" the reporter asked.

The smiling faces of Nathalie and Kessler were replaced bit by bit by another image.

Jason fiddled with the cable, pounded on the monitor, and suddenly the picture came into focus. Jason stared at a hideous green face with no nose. He saw a lipless mouth lined with bone-white teeth. Bright red eyes blazed beneath beetled brows. Towering above those awful orbs was a bulging braincase three times the size of a human head. Veins pulsed. Fluids dribbled.

Jason gasped. "What's that?"

★ ★ ★ ★

Earth

That was the question of the moment.

Nathalie West's voice told the American public that her picture signal was jammed. The image on-screen was being broadcast from beyond the Earth.

In the Luxor, Byron Williams murmured, "That's a Martian."

In the White House, Taffy Dale said exactly same words at the same time. She was deeply intrigued, which was more than could be said for her mother. The First Lady was appalled. "I do not want that *thing* in my house."

Neither did the First Dog, Rusty. The big golden retriever barked at the Martian's image on the TV screen.

President Dale negotiated. "We might have to invite them. People will expect me to meet with them."

His wife laid down her terms. "Well, they're not eating off the Van Buren china."

The creature on the screen clicked its teeth. Obviously, it was speaking, but the earthly audience was too shocked by its Halloween-mask face to hear.

Poppy barked fiercely at a *Today in Fashion* monitor. Nathalie West sought comfort in Donald's strong arms. She exclaimed, "Ugh! It's gross!"

"Don't forget, Nathalie. We look equally *gross* to a Martian," Kessler pointed out.

Nathalie's face lit with sudden understanding. "Oh, yeah, like the blonde niece on *The Munsters*."

In the Perkinsville donut shop, Richie gaped at the Martian's humongous head. "Look at that brain! He must be really smart!"

The hideous creature bowed and drew a circle in the air.

Richie put down his donut and turned to Rosie. "Whoa! He made the international sign of the donut!"

Then the Martian disappeared.

★ ★ ★

Thursday, May 11—3:45 P.M.
Washington, D.C.

Professor Kessler had seen enough to draw a few conclusions, along with some complicated charts. From his limited data, the good professor had made three inferences: "One: Our Martian friend is a carbon-based life form. Two: He breathes nitrogen. Three: The large cerebrum indicates telepathic potential." Kessler's laser pointer rested on the alien's bulging brain.

Jerry Ross was seriously disturbed by this theory. "You mean they can read our thoughts?"

"Potentially, yes," Kessler asserted.

Jerry broke into a sweat. He hated the Martians already. The other men in the room murmured. Evidently, the idea of telepathy disturbed them too.

General Decker scowled. A Martian wouldn't like what it read in *his* thoughts.

President Dale shuddered. Politics and

telepathy were a dangerous mix! Creatures who could read thoughts would never make good voters. His career was doomed! Unless he could get a Martian to work for him. . . .

Affable General Casey believed telepathy would promote understanding. Unfortunately, he had no understanding of the true nature of the Martians.

There was another man in the room, Dr. Wolfgang Ziegler. The eminent Dr. Ziegler was a man of deep learning and a shadowy past. He declined to shed light on his whereabouts prior to 1950. He also kept his funding secret.

Dr. Ziegler was making final adjustments on his greatest achievement: an electronic translator. With his own hands, Ziegler had assembled the hardware. And with his genius, he had created the software to run it. Ziegler's translator had already broken the Martian language into 227 phonemes, 48 diphthongs, and 292 other sounds in a 4.5 octave range.

Let Kessler spout his theories about the green foreigners. Ziegler would make it possible for mankind to communicate with the alien swine! The translator was a scientific achievement to surpass all others! This was his destiny!

Kessler repeated his belief that the Martians' high level of technology indicated an advanced culture. In his logic, advanced cultures were peaceful and enlightened. Kessler said, "The human race, on the other hand, is a dangerously aggressive species."

His voice choked with emotion, Kessler concluded, "I suspect they have more to fear from us than we from them."

The professor paused and stepped to the side. "Doctor?"

Ziegler straightened up and turned around. He spoke in a measured accent. "Thank you, professor. I have run the Martian transmission through seven different linguistics programs. The results are not perfect, but this may answer some of your questions."

He tapped a key. The strange voice of the Martian was heard. Ziegler made adjustments. Tapes revolved. Lights flashed. And then the translator croaked: "All green of skin, eight hundred centuries ago. Their bodily fluids include the birth of half-breeds."

"How many centuries ago?" the President

quavered. He was trying to take notes. He didn't want anyone to think he was . . . well, not on top of things. But this didn't make sense.

The translator said, "For dark is the suede that mows like a harvest."

Decker growled, "What does that mean?"

Dr. Ziegler scratched his head. There were always problems. Ziegler would fix them. The fools would yet see his invention triumph. They would hear the words of the Martians and finally know why they had come.

But it would be too late. . . .

★ ★ ★

Las Vegas, Nevada

Barbara Land was sure she knew why the Martians had come. She stood before an Alcoholics Anonymous meeting. Barbara looked over the crummy meeting hall and the cloud of smoke drifting under the ceiling. Twenty or so shabby folding chairs seated a sorry band. The recovering alcoholics slumped and slouched and puffed cigarettes.

Yet in this dismal place, Barbara felt tingly all over. "Hello, my name is Barbara," she chirped.

"Hello, Barbara," the smokers chanted.

"I'm an alcoholic, but I haven't had a drink in three months," Barbara confessed to bored applause.

Then she felt the spirit move her. And she told the sad people everything Art refused to hear. Barbara said she felt optimistic, because we weren't alone in the universe anymore. Our planet was suffering from holes in the ozone and dying forests, and people were unhappy in their lives. "And here at the beginning of a new millennium the Martians heard our global cry for help!"

Barbara looked into the shining eyes of her audience. "People say they're ugly. But I think the Martians are here to show us the way! They've come to save us!"

The crowd cheered.

★ ★ ★ ★

Perkinsville, Kansas

The Norris family cheered its hero, Billy-Glenn. He was dressed in his freshly pressed uniform with the private stripe gleaming on the sleeve. The family stood at the bus stop in the heart of Perkinsville.

A bus purred like a big metal cat. The dusty air stank of diesel exhaust. Billy-Glenn tossed his duffel bag into the baggage hold. His mother hugged him.

His girlfriend, Kelly, drawled, "Be careful, baby. Don't get killed or anything." She sniffled.

Big Glenn clapped his elder son firmly on the back. "We're real proud of you, son. Perkinsville's finest."

Richie shook his brother's hand. He could hardly believe Billy-Glenn was leaving, even when he said, "So long, retard. Just don't touch my stuff while I'm gone."

Billy-Glenn kissed Kelly. And Mom cried some more. Grandma got mixed up about who was leaving. Then everybody said, "Bye, bye, bye," and the bus door squealed shut. The bus rumbled away.

Richie sighed, "Well, he's gone for a while."

Kelly choked back a sob.

Sue-Ann said, "Oh, Richie, why can't you be more like your brother?"

"We was lucky with Billy-Glenn," Dad said grimly. He spit on the ground. "You can't expect the same luck twice."

Dad was always saying stuff like that. He had for as long as Richie could remember, which wasn't very long. But Dad was always doing that. And Richie knew he was sort of useless. Dad said it, and he was never wrong. Many's the time Dad had said Richie was just as useless as Grandma. And Grandma was really useless.

But Richie had dreams. He thought that someday, he had no idea how this might happen, but someday, he was going to do something really cool.

Richie stared gloomily at the ground. His Dad grunted. "Want to do something useful? Take Grandma back to the home."

Richie liked Grandma, so that was no problem. He got the old lady strapped into the red pickup, and they were bouncing down the road in no time.

Richie was excited. He wondered if Grandma had ever thought she would see Martians come to Earth. He bet she'd seen all kinds of far-out stuff in her life.

But Grandma wasn't interested. She said, "I want to get back to Slim and Muffy and Richie."

"I'm Richie," her grandson said.

"I know. Richie was the best one," Grandma said vaguely.

Richie sighed. This was like talking to a Martian.

Almost as bad as talking to Dad. Richie didn't think his father was really mean. Glenn just saw things Glenn's way. And Richie was . . . Richie. Glenn and Sue-Ann couldn't imagine anything outside their point of view.

Glenn thought Richie was spaced out. Richie was just trying to keep a wider perspective on things. Like at the end of some cartoons, when the camera zooms out farther and farther, until the Earth is this small dot floating alone in space. Only now we were not alone.

Richie drove past a row of power pylons marching across the land like a line of giant robots. Because these huge towers had transformers,

Richie had always thought of them as kids' toys, like Autobots and Decepticons. Whenever he saw them, he knew he was approaching the Lawrence Welk Retirement Village.

When he arrived at the Retirement Village, a nice nurse helped Richie put Grandma in a wheelchair. They rolled her through a lounge filled with old people watching TV.

This totally mellow music oozed out of the speakers. This stuff was way too mellow for Richie. Why would people want to listen to mall music if they weren't even shopping?

Richie tried not to notice the old-people smell as they cruised the hallway to Grandma's room. They even popped a couple of wheelies on the way.

Grandma had a pretty good room. She could see the garden, which was cool except for being cluttered up with geezers. And she had all her stuff here, including her favorite cat, Muffy. Which was a righteous piece of taxidermy but kind of creepy. Grandma still liked to talk to Muffy. Richie wondered if Muffy heard somehow, or if she was sleeping. That's about all the cat ever did when she was alive.

While Richie thanked the nurse, Grandma wheeled herself over to an old-fashioned record player and plugged in headphones.

Richie said, "Grandma, if you need any donuts or anything, call me, okay?"

Grandma's trembling hands dropped the tone arm of the record player. The needle hit the groove in her favorite record: *Slim Whitman and His Singing Guitar, Volume Two.*

Bliss spread over Grandma's wrinkled face as she lost herself in memory.

★ ★ ★

Las Vegas, Nevada

In his drab little apartment, Byron Williams was reviewing some memories too. He leafed through an old scrapbook, proud of the posters and photos of past bouts. He'd fought with the best: Frazier, Ali, Norton. And sometimes he'd won.

He swigged a soda and washed down the remains of a microwave meal. Byron didn't like the last clipping in the scrapbook: "Ex-Champ Arrested for Spousal Abuse."

That was a bad time. Byron deeply regretted everything he had done. He would never act like that again. He was a changed man. The only way to show Louise was to straighten out those boys. But he didn't have the money to get to Washington.

Byron went for a jog to clear his head. He hadn't gone far when he realized a dark limo was trailing him. Byron wasn't afraid of much, so he stopped, and the limo stopped. The window rolled down, and Byron saw Art Land's crafty grin.

Just out of curiosity, Byron accepted the ride. But he didn't accept Art's deal. Of course Art had a deal. He always had a deal. Smooth as a devil, he tempted Byron with the kind of money he needed to fly back to Washington and take care of his family. But Byron knew that a man like Art Land always came out on top of any deal. Accepting an offer from him was asking for trouble.

Oh, he buttered Byron up pretty well, but a man who has fought in the ring has too much pride to swing his fist for some sleazy hood. That was gangster stuff. Byron wasn't going to make a mistake like that again.

"I found God, and I'm a better man. I've tamed that bull, and I don't want to bring him out," Byron told Art.

The big-time operator dropped Byron off at the next corner. He could buy other muscle. To Art Land, Byron was just a chump, not a champ.

★ ★ ★

Saturday, May 13—4:58 A.M.
The White House

"Hey, you want to keep it down? People live here," Taffy scolded General Decker. She slouched in the door of her bedroom.

Decker did not apologize for yelling at this time of night. He merely growled at President Dale's slack-jawed slacker kid. The man couldn't even control his own smart-mouthed brat. How could he control the country?

The President had just finished an emergency

press conference. Decker was furious because, in his very loud opinion, the country was in the hands of half-wits. That bottom-feeding creep Jerry Ross played patty-cake with the press. And then the President gassed on for another fifteen minutes. The reporters asked stupid questions like Do the Martians use money? and Are there male and female Martians?

The President was treating this like any other foreign policy situation. He wanted to chitchat with monsters!

Then the hideous Martians sent landing coordinates. They were expected to touch down in the Nevada desert at a place called Pahrump. Did President Dale want troops there? No! He sent Casey to hand out daisies. And that blasted Brit Kessler really iced Decker's cake when he said, "We need a welcome mat, not a row of tanks."

If you asked Decker, the professor was a welcome mat, and the Martians were going to wipe their feet on him.

★ ★ ★ ★

Saturday, May 13
Pahrump, Nevada

One day can change history. The day that would change Earth's history forever began as a beautiful spring morning. Under a cloudless blue sky the Nevada desert was green with new life. Northeast of the Martian coordinates was the infamous Area 51, rumored for years to be the secret hiding place of a captured flying saucer. To the west lay the Amargosa mountains, and beyond them, Death Valley. A little to the south was the town of Pahrump, a delightful green oasis with casinos and golf courses.

Today, the little city was swamped. The roads swarmed with traffic. People parked in the desert and hurried to the landing site. Already the air vibrated with an unearthly throbbing.

The army prepared the landing site as quickly as if this were a planned maneuver. The Martian landing coordinates were surrounded by a ring of whirring helicopters. Soldiers quickly erected a barrier fence. Another detail had assembled a stage. A military band took their instruments from their cases and tuned up.

General Casey had provided for the presence of the media. Vans from many television networks flanked the fence.

Jason Stone talked to technicians at the GNN van. He and Nathalie had just flown in from New York. Jason felt keyed up and jet-lagged at the same time. His hair was still flat from the flight.

Jason was just a little worried about the way Nathalie talked about Dr. Kessler. He tried to put that out of his mind. He was going to cover a historic occasion! This was for the greater glory of GNN.

Jason heard the throbbing and looked up. Were the Martians here already? Jason hoped he had time to check his hair.

Nathalie West looked up too. She hoped the other Martian effects would be as awesome as the sound. These guys were rockin'! She adjusted her hat against the desert wind.

Nathalie slipped Poppy into her pocket. The Chihuahua was a bit peeved, and so was Nathalie. The network had called in the middle of the night and flown her out to Babump, or whatever this pit was called. Nathalie was missing an important sale at Barney's. And now her appointment book was all messed up.

But it was kind of cute that Jason's network called too. Nathalie was so glad they could have a his 'n' hers Martian landing. She figured this would be great for her Q rating. After all, everyone in the world was watching.

And while they watched, a flying disk grew bigger and bigger in the sky.

Even the President was glued to his tube. Dale had wanted to attend the landing himself. But his security people insisted he stay home. Instead, Dale, Marsha, and Taffy would be present in spirit only, watching the landing on television like every other American.

However, some Americans had traveled long distances to be at this historic event. Some were driven by curiosity, and some, like Barbara Land, were on a quest for the truth. She felt good vibes in Pahrump, and not just because the name came from the Shoshone Indian words for "deep waters."

Barbara carefully arranged candles and crystals in a circle on the hood of her Mercedes. Then she sat cross-legged in Lotus position in the circle's center. Barbara reached out her arms, looked up at the sky, and prepared to receive the wisdom of the space beings. She chanted her mantra in time to the cosmic throbbing in the sky.

The sound of clumsy hammering disturbed Barbara's trance. Nearby, Billy-Glenn Norris, private first class, pounded a fence post into the sandy Nevada soil. His detail had already erected a row of flags and a giant banner: WELCOME TO EARTH.

Billy-Glenn was sorely disappointed. His moment of glory was suspiciously like every other moment of his army career. He had always been either digging, peeling, or hammering. It was altogether too much like chores at home, but without the free stale donuts.

Billy-Glenn glanced over and saw General Casey's honor guard. They looked like perfect toy soldiers. Billy-Glenn wished he could make honor guard someday. He bet those guys didn't dig.

Billy-Glenn almost smashed his thumb when he caught sight of the enormous flying saucer blotting out the sun. It was huge!

The massive Martian disk slowed almost to a stop in midair before unfolding crablike legs. The throbbing changed into a whirring whine. The army helicopters were forced to lift off to give the vast saucer room to touch down.

This was the day General Casey had worked for all his life. Now he could show the whole world the glory of the United States Army.

The weather was perfect. His orders had been carried out to the letter. The men were alert and majestic, with a snap in their step. His officers had been carefully briefed to treat the Martians as foreign dignitaries. Here was the greatest moment in human history, and Casey was at the bat.

The general turned to Dr. Ziegler and was assured there would be no trouble with the translator. Casey couldn't resist making a triumphant call to his wife.

"I get to greet the Martian Ambassador! Isn't that great? It's a heck of an honor," he gushed. "Didn't I always tell you, honey, if I stayed in line and I didn't speak out, good things would happen?"

The saucer's landing legs gripped the ground. The whine went up in pitch and then faded.

Jason Stone murmured in a breathless voice, as

if he were at a funeral, or describing a golf match: "Teeming masses gathered here from who knows how many states. Have they come out of curiosity, hope for change, for progress, adventure, or something to tell their grand-children? Or just to say, 'I was there'? I was there when man first met with Martian. This is Jason Stone. GNN. Pahrump."

Nathalie's take was completely different. This was *Today in Fashion.* Where Jason saw history in the making, Nathalie saw a festival. There was plenty of long hair and tie-dye in the crowd. Too bad Casey wasn't hip enough to book Smashing Pumpkins instead of that tacky oompah-pah band.

Nathalie chattered to the camera until a spaceship hatch opened. She squealed, "A ramp is emerging like a silver tongue."

General Casey gasped. "Gee whiz!"

Then, for a moment, no one uttered a sound. Down the silver ramp glided the Martian Ambassador. His tall, gaunt green form was draped in a glinting crimson cloak. A shiny dome protected his mammoth brain matter. The Ambassador's red eyes surveyed the Earthlings.

A dozen of Mars's finest marched in rows on either side of their awesome Ambassador. These green creatures' long legs and arms were ringed with jointed metal tubing. Their chests were crisscrossed with flexible hoses that joined domed helmets to life-support backpacks. The Martians carried toylike contraptions of tubes and spheres.

Banners snapped in the breeze. Sunlight gleamed on polished metal. With enormous dignity, General Casey stepped forward and extended his hand.

The Martian Ambassador folded his arms. He seemed suspicious, even hostile. His scarlet eyes blazed. His noseless, lipless face seemed set in a snarl.

Then General Casey drew a big circle in the air.

The Martian Ambassador relaxed and spoke.

"Wait! Wait one second, please!" Dr. Ziegler begged. He pushed buttons and twirled knobs. The scientist adjusted his masterpiece for frequency as well as meaning. The red Martian eyes obviously saw in a foreign frequency of light, and their small ears were tuned to strange wavelengths.

Ziegler's translator repeated in its flat, robotic tones: "Greetings. I am the Martian Ambassador."

With everything in phase, General Casey responded, "Greetings. I am General Casey, Commanding Officer of the Armed Forces of the United States of America. On behalf of the people of Earth, welcome!"

There was a small pause as the translator turned Casey's speech into Martian. Then the Ambassador's many teeth clicked and chattered. The translator droned: "We come in peace. We come in peace. We come in peace."

The crowd was delighted. Applause rippled and swelled. A happy hippie released a white dove. People laughed and cheered, and applauded all the louder when the dove fluttered over the Martian Ambassador.

The Martian rolled his great red eyes, lifted an odd device, and *blasted the bird to oblivion*! Before its charred feathers could hit the ground, the Martians leveled their ray guns at the crowd.

People's ears were pierced by unfamiliar frequencies of energy. Their eyes were dazzled by blazing bursts of photons and particles in exotic combinations. The product of strange energies and weird science, the humming ray guns shot out molten blooms of fire!

General Casey, his officers, and guards were cut down in a blinding flash. Ribbons of fire were flung over the crowd. Screaming victims fled through swirling smoke and exploding tanks. A flaming helicopter spun down into the panicked mob.

The polite parade had instantly turned into a blazing battleground. Grinning Martians torched everything that moved. The Ambassador turned and strode up the spaceship ramp. His blood-red cloak swirled behind him.

Billy-Glenn Norris recovered his wits just in time to see a ghastly Martian stalking past him. Dazed as he was, Billy-Glenn whipped out his pistol and screamed, "Die! You alien butthead!"

All of Billy-Glenn's hours of training paid off. His aim was calm, cool, and steady. He popped off a whole clip before he realized the bullets were just bouncing off the Martian's sleek body armor. PING PING PING PING.

The Martian turned its grisly face to look at him. Billy-Glenn's gun was empty. He thought faster than he ever had in his life. Billy-Glenn

Norris grabbed an American flag and offered it to the invader. He said sheepishly, "Uh, I surrender."

The Martian lifted his ray gun, and Billy-Glenn, gripping the flag, went out in a blaze of Old Glory. A GNN cameraman captured the scene.

KA-BOOM! An explosion rocked the media vans.

Nathalie was thrown to the ground. Jason leaped to join her. He cried, "Nathalie! Nathalie!"

When her eyes opened, Jason thanked the Good Lord. At that moment, nothing else seemed to matter. Kessler didn't matter. The Pulitzer Prize didn't matter. Not even his hair mattered. Nathalie was alive! They were together. Jason tenderly took her hand.

And then a Martian ray struck Jason. Nathalie saw him go out of focus like a B-movie optical! Jason's flesh *evaporated*! The body that was going to fill that new Barney's suit was . . . gone!

Nathalie screamed as a Martian grabbed her and Poppy. She was being abducted by aliens!

Barbara Land felt betrayed by the universe. Here in Pahrump, the bright promise of a Golden

Age had been reduced to a smoldering graveyard.

Thick, black, greasy smoke rolled off the charred bandstand and the field of steaming skeletons. Barbara could not stop weeping. She had witnessed the unthinkable. And she was not alone. The whole world had watched what happens when Mars attacks.

Washington, D.C.

"Did you see that? Did you see that?" President Dale was deeply shocked. Everything had been fine. The setting was perfect. The band was in tune. The men looked great. Dale thought that Casey delivered a wonderful speech. His drawing a circle in the air was genius! The dove was also a nice touch. The audience loved it. Dale suspected Jerry Ross needed a pat on the back for that Kodak moment. So what went wrong?

Everyone in the room talked at once. Decker had the military on full alert. The general wanted to nuke the Martians. Even the First Lady wanted to kick their asteroids.

Jerry Ross thought they ought to get a public opinion poll. He was very upset. He'd planned to take credit for that dove thing. And now the situation called for some major spin control.

Jerry surfed channels to see how news people were reacting. The trouble with fast-breaking disasters was the risk of not choosing the right opinion. Nukes would be the no-nonsense, decisive move. But the public had a negative attitude toward global destruction. So far, the surviving anchors were just stammering and weeping. On CNBC there were only pictures, no commentary. Jerry bit his lip. This was going to be tough.

Kessler cautioned, "I know this is terrible. But please don't be rash. That dove frightened them."

Taffy agreed. "Yeah. Maybe on Mars doves mean war."

"Look! Carl Sagan!" Jerry exclaimed. The eminent astronomer was telling talk-show host Larry King that he believed the Martian behavior was a mistake.

Sagan's measured tones reassured billions and

billions of listeners. "If you'll review the footage, Larry, you'll see the Martians react adversely to the sound of people clapping. For us, applause is a sign of approval and support. But to the Martians it may be offensive, a sign of aggression if you will. Symbols are not universal. For example, among the hill tribes of New Guinea, if you smile it means you're sad, and if you frown you're happy."

Everyone in the White House was frowning. And they weren't happy. President Dale wondered if Sagan, Kessler, and Taffy were right. He couldn't let the Martians' hideous appearance influence his decision.

Clearly the Martians had highly advanced technology. Earth's crude weapons were primitive compared with the Martian arsenal. Risking war would be foolhardy. The odds were in the Martians' favor. There was only one way to come out on top in this situation: Make friends. The massacre must have been a cultural misunderstanding. The Martians *did* say, "We come in peace."

That night, after hours of painful indecision, President James Dale broadcast a secret message to the Martians. He invited the Ambassador to sit

down in friendship, to reason together. Dale only hoped the Martians wouldn't chip the Van Buren china, or Marsha would kill him.

★ ★ ★

Space

The Martian command spaceship was a dark and gloomy place. Instrument panels and indicators on strange machines blinked and whirled in the faint red light. But Nathalie was sure she was in some kind of laboratory, just like those poor people on *Oprah*.

Those UFO abductees were always whining about being stuck with needles and peculiar instruments. The Martians had plenty of those. But right now, the aliens were busy staring at the image of the American presidential seal on a giant TV screen.

They seemed to be fascinated by birds. But who could tell what they were up to? The Martians barely had faces, much less expressions.

Nathalie floated in her underwear in a giant

glass egg. She held Poppy in her arms.

There were other glass eggs holding biological specimens: a cow, a giant squid, a pig, a sheep, a camel, and a clown. Through the gummy liquid, Nathalie could dimly see Martian scientists poking thin rods into the charred dove. Beyond them, a nerdy Martian operated some kind of communications gear.

Nathalie expected to see Rod Serling come around the corner. Wasn't it time for *Unsolved Mysteries* to go to commercial break?

Nathalie had thought the inside of a spaceship would be very different. This looked more like a college fraternity house than a vessel of doom. But Nathalie had been with the Martians long enough to know they were weird. They weren't like Darth Vader or Klingons or anything. They were more like nasty little boys with dangerous toys.

A Martian came close to her egg and touched some buttons. Nathalie blacked out for a while.

When she came to, she thought she was having an out-of-body experience. There she was in her underwear on this Martian operating table with a lot of tubes and stuff sticking out of her. It was totally *Outer Limits*.

But, wait, call the *X-Files*! Nathalie wasn't having an out-of-body experience! One of the Martians moved, and she saw Poppy's bulging eyes and yapping muzzle swiveling on a tiny neck between *Nathalie's shoulders*!!!

It was too weird! Nathalie was just a head in a jar! It was such a bummer she had to scream.

★ ★ ★

Monday, May 15—9:07 A.M.
Perkinsville, Kansas

Richie couldn't get over it. Just a few days ago, Billy-Glenn was getting on the bus, and now he had come back in the baggage compartment. And there were all these dudes around town. There were reporters and photographers and all kinds of strangers.

Richie's boss didn't want to let him off from the donut shop. Business was booming. But Richie reminded him that he was Billy-Glenn's brother, and the boss almost gave him a medal. It was weird.

There were pictures of Billy-Glenn everywhere, all over the tube, on all the newspapers. Everywhere you looked you saw a flaming Billy-Glenn grabbing the flag from the clutching claws of a gruesome green Martian. He was the hero of the Pahrump Massacre. He was part of an event, like that tea party in Boston, the Alamo, or Woodstock. Billy-Glenn was going to be in the history books. Richie couldn't believe his brother was suddenly famous, dead, and extra crispy.

Richie wore his best clothes and stood with the rest of the family in the Perkinsville cemetery. Grandma snoozed in her wheelchair. Kelly was all in black and sobbing.

There were tons of dudes cramming the graveyard—people Richie had never seen in Perkinsville. A lot of them wore Pahrump Massacre T-shirts.

A flag covered the coffin. There were army dudes with white gloves and bugles, and a twenty-one-gun salute, which was really deafening!

"Why did it have to be him?" Glenn asked the heavens in a manly voice. He made sure he was in plain sight of all the TV cameras perched like buzzards on their operators' shoulders.

Dad looked brave and Mom was crying, just the way they were supposed to. It was like a movie. Some stranger said, "Imagine dyin' while fightin' for our flag."

"There ain't many heroes," another stranger agreed.

Richie thought, *Who are all these people?* Then he figured maybe they were the extras in the movie.

Dad barely spoke to Richie during the whole funeral, like he was ticked off or something. Richie sighed. Now he really had something to live up to. Billy-Glenn was a national hero. Billy-Glenn was a best-selling T-shirt!

★ ★ ★ ★

Washington, D.C.

Louise made breakfast and watched Billy-Glenn's funeral on the TV in her kitchen. Cedric and Neville were in the living room vaporizing invaders on their video game.

When Byron called, Louise worried that something was wrong. But he sounded as eager as a kid and ready to see her tomorrow at four when the plane came in.

She let the boys chatter with their dad about their game and school. They were most excited about their school trip to the White House.

"I guess this means you're still making it to school once in a while," Byron joked. Then he asked to speak to Louise again.

"What are you wasting the phone time for?" she wondered. "We'll see you tomorrow."

Louise was always so practical. Byron blurted, "I just had to tell you that I love you."

Louise was surprised and faintly alarmed at how good those words sounded. "I love you too, Byron. Now stop wasting money. I'll see you tomorrow."

Louise found herself humming as she finished breakfast. She had something to look forward to. All was right with the world.

★

The Martian response to the President's message had come in the wee hours of the morning. Jerry Ross was ecstatic. "They've issued a formal apology! The Martian Ambassador feels terrible and asks permission to speak to Congress."

James Dale felt vindicated. This was a major victory for his administration. He had averted the first interplanetary war. Maybe they'd name an interplanetary holiday after him, or at least give him his own postage stamp.

Every effort was made to ensure that the next meeting with the Martians went smoothly. A huge crowd gathered around the Capitol building. Police patrolled the streets to prevent angry acts of revenge against the alien visitors.

On the steps leading up to the great colonnade, one cop held up a sign: NO BIRDS. Another officer displayed a sign that read: NO APPLAUSE.

The eerie, throbbing whir of a Martian saucer arrived on the fresh spring breeze. The giant disk dwarfed the Capitol dome. People started to clap at the glorious sight, then remembered they shouldn't. So they laughed and watched the disk make a perfect landing on the Capitol lawn. The crablike legs gently clutched the green grass. The saucer was down.

Once again, flags flew and bands played. Despite the recent disaster, there was a holiday mood. People in the crowd barely noticed the row of tanks parked discreetly to one side of the lawn.

Sitting in an open tank hatch, an angry General Decker glared through field glasses at the Capitol dome. Decker had thrown a tantrum to be allowed his little "welcome mat." He felt as if his hands were tied by his own leader and the enemy was laughing at them. But the beasts wouldn't be laughing once Decker fired. No, his time would come. The army would prove itself.

Inside the Capitol building, Donald Kessler was also sure that the day's events would prove him right. The scientist shared the podium with the ancient southern Speaker of the House.

Kessler observed the Martians waiting to step up on the stage. He theorized that their armor was not military in nature, but served to support them against Earth's gravity. After all, our planet's pull on muscle and bone was nearly twice that of Mars.

The Speaker drawled his way through a rambling introduction. "This is a proud day for all Americans, and especially for my good friends in Tennessee's fifth district. Now, if y'all will quiet down, the Martian Ambassador is going to say a few words. Come on up, Mr. Ambassador."

Once again, President Dale watched the historic events unfold on television. He was upset to miss this stupendous photo-op. Jerry reminded him that the Secret Service had been right about Pahrump. It wouldn't be a good idea to put the executive branch and the legislative branch in the same place at the same time.

The Ambassador and his guards had reached the podium. Banks of television cameras followed the monstrous Martians' every move. Members of Congress tried to look dignified. But fear and disgust flashed in their eyes and twisted their mouths. Humans were instinctively repulsed by the death's-head faces and quivering cerebrums of the grotesque extraterrestrials.

They all shuddered under the piercing gaze of the Ambassador's fiery scarlet eyes. Bony fingers reached under the crimson cloak. Congress inhaled in one collective gasp.

But the Ambassador merely withdrew a scrolled speech. A polite murmur of relieved laughter rippled over Congress.

The Ambassador mimed laughter and looked at his troopers. When he turned back to the humans, he held a ray gun! So did all the guards. They fired!

As unknown, deadly energies raked the room, Kessler fell to his knees. He pleaded with the Martian Ambassador. "Please! What are you doing? This isn't logical! This doesn't make—"

Whap!

One of the Martians clubbed Kessler with his ray gun.

The quiet of the hall was shattered by screams and the unearthly whine of Martian weapons. The ancient wooden paneling smoldered. Distinguished statesmen collapsed into heaps of seared bones. Then the television cameras were engulfed in flames. And the picture went out.

Taffy stared at the static on the screen. "I guess it wasn't the dove."

"Not again!" President Dale wailed. At this rate, he would never be reelected. He could just kiss his career good-bye. He was going to be the laughingstock of history—if anyone lived to write history.

Smoke billowed out of the Capitol dome, and

the Martians slithered down the stone steps, ray guns fizzing. Bystanders fled in terror from the lethal rays. Skeletons littered the marble plaza. The Martians strolled coolly to their waiting saucer.

General Decker had his chance at last! He screamed orders into a mobile phone. Decker commanded his tanks to open fire! The Washington mall echoed with the rapid RATATATAT of light weapons over the bass boom of tank cannons.

Billy-Glenn could have told Decker the bullets would do no good. PING PING PING. They bounced off the Martian armor. The creatures didn't even slow down as they ran up the ramp. As the saucer took off, shells popped harmlessly against its shiny hull. In seconds, the disk whisked out of sight.

Decker shook his fist and screamed, "And stay out!"

★ ★ ★

Space

Eventually, Nathalie stopped screaming. The Martians didn't care, and it was just making a lot of bubbles in her jar.

Besides, Nathalie was the kind of person who made the best of things. Number one, she was still alive. Number two, just when she was getting very bored with sitting on a shelf, the Martians brought in the adorable Dr. Kessler, whom they had taken from the Capitol building.

Nathalie was sure that her dream-date scientist would find a way to get back her bodacious bod, so she could get her head together. Then maybe they could swing on a rope while he was shooting a death ray, like the heroes did in *Star Wars* or James Bond movies.

Unfortunately, life isn't like the movies. Donald didn't do any of that stuff. The medical Martians took him apart. And somehow, each and every part was alive in a jar!

Nathalie fared only slightly better. The next time she awoke, she had a body again. Too bad it was Poppy's! And Nathalie really needed to take a walk.

Kessler finally came around. He looked pained as he realized his situation. Then his eyes settled on Nathalie's jar.

"Nathalie, is that you?" Donald sounded like he hadn't a care in the world now that he was with her.

Nathalie fought the urge to bite an itchy place on her hind leg. "How are you feeling?"

The British scientist kept a stiff upper lip. It was about all he had left. "Not terribly good, I'm afraid."

"Can I ask you a question?" Nathalie ventured, trying to keep her tail from wagging too much. *Be cool, girl!*

"Yes, of course," Kessler replied.

"Were you flirting with me on the show? Because if you were, I just want you to know I liked it," Nathalie confessed.

"You did, really?" Kessler gushed. "Because, you know, I've watched you on TV quite a bit, and, well, I've had something of a schoolboy crush on you for, gosh, ages."

Nathalie beamed. She couldn't help herself. Her wagging tail nearly thumped her jar off the shelf.

★ ★ ★

Washington, D.C.

"It seems I owe you an apology, General," President Dale said wearily. The war room was grim with the aftermath of this second atrocity.

Jerry Ross was stressed out beyond belief. This wasn't spin control, it was orbit control! Jerry hated to hear his boss making nice with Decker. He gritted his teeth when Decker said smugly, "We all make mistakes, Mr. President."

James Dale banged his fist on the table. "Well, not anymore. We're going to take charge of this thing."

Jerry made a mental note to remind the President to use that gesture in his next speech. It looked great!

Decker had anticipated this moment. He had already prepared the orders. All he needed was the President's signature. Then he could make full use of the nation's nuclear deterrent. He'd show those skull-faced . . .

"Are you out of your mind?" the President

asked. He put down Decker's papers, unsigned. "I'm not going to start a war."

"The war's already started!" Decker declared. "We've got to nuke 'em now!"

Jerry shook his head. This looked bad for the reelection. Heck, it looked bad just for staying in office!

Dale told Decker that if he didn't shut up he would be relieved of his command. The general was stunned, but he always obeyed orders.

The President had orders for Jerry and his staff. He wanted a cop on every corner. He wanted America to know that schools were still open and the garbage would be picked up. Dale wanted them to know they still had two out of three branches of government working for them.

The President wasted no time going on television to announce his grave decision: The United States would suspend diplomatic relations with the Martians.

★

It had been a rough day. But Jerry felt it was finally all in hand. The Martians hadn't returned. The people seemed to accept the congressional massacre.

Jerry needed some stress relief, the kind that even golf couldn't provide.

As he walked to his limo, he saw just what he needed. A beautiful young woman with a tall beehive hairdo stood just outside the White House gates.

Jerry really liked the woman's gown. It looked like a European design. She also wore a large, unusual ring on her finger.

The smooth press secretary didn't hesitate for a minute. He walked right over to her and offered a personalized tour of the White House. The ploy worked every time, and it didn't fail him now.

She nodded. The young woman did not speak. Her jaws steadily chewed a piece of very blue gum.

Jerry figured she was from Sweden or someplace exotic. He didn't care if she didn't speak English, as long as she wanted to party.

In moments, Jerry and the woman were standing in the shadows of the colonnade. He tapped on French doors. His friend Mitch, the Secret Service man, let them in.

Jerry began his usual pitch. Women loved hearing all about the White House. But this one didn't seem to care about the paintings or which room was decorated by which First Lady. And after Taffy walked by and made a sarcastic remark about "the midnight tour," Jerry decided to show his new friend the secret room.

He pressed a button, and a bookcase turned into a bar. Jerry mixed some drinks while the woman studied objects in the room: a fish tank and a little bronze statue. Jerry felt the time was right for romance.

Just before he kissed the girl, he asked her to take the gum out of her mouth. She didn't seem to understand, so Jerry gently plucked at the gum. The girl bit him! She bit very hard!

Then she spit out Jerry's finger!

Jerry screamed. He pulled at the girl's cheek. To his horror, her human cheek came off, revealing Martian skin and teeth beneath!

Jerry moaned and grabbed a telephone. He dialed 911.

Choking and gasping, the girl picked up the little bronze statue and whacked Jerry's head with it. His troubles were over.

The girl desperately searched her purse for a fresh stick of bright blue gum. Once it was in her mouth, her breathing returned to normal. Then she calmly took a ray gun from her purse. She was a special Martian assassin.

Ray gun in hand, the creature crept down the dark, carpeted halls of the White House. She broke a heel off her shoe. When she bent down to fix it, a Secret Service man spotted her. Before he could react, the ray gun zapped, and he fell dead.

The ruthless assassin soon found the doorway to the President's bedroom. She could see the President's dog, Rusty, sleeping at the foot of the President's bed.

The assassin scratched at her head. Then she pulled off her beehive, revealing a giant brain, and peeled off the rubber face.

The Martian activated a tiny camera concealed in her bulky ring. The device was a direct link to the Martian command ship. The Martian leader liked to see enemy leaders meet their doom.

The assassin took careful aim. Just then, Rusty woke. He leaped up and began to bark, startling the Martians watching the monitor on the command ship.

The assassin fired, and a line of flames sprang up between the President and the First Lady. The dog's jaws clamped down on the assassin's thigh.

The First Lady screamed! The President slapped a security alarm.

The Martian kicked Rusty across the room. She reduced the beast to bones with her deadly ray, then took aim at the President.

Whap! Rusty's skull bounced off the Martian's head. The First Lady's desperate pitch had saved her husband. The President struggled with the Martian.

Mitch burst through the door. "Don't shoot!" he cautioned the other White House guards. The Martian put her ray gun to Dale's head and backed out a second door.

She dragged the President into a dressing room, where she bumped into a covered bird cage. The cloth slipped off, and a small parakeet squawked in fear.

Alarmed, the Martian fried the bird. And Mitch had his chance. "Get down!" he screamed. The President dropped to the floor. BLAM BLAM BLAM! Mitch's pistol barked. The assassin fell, and the President was splattered with slime and green gook.

"Thanks, Mitch," Dale said.

The Secret Serviceman replied soberly, "It's my job."

★ ★ ★ ★

Space

The Martian leader was in a fine fury. The puny Earth beings had killed his favorite assassin. He had been denied the pleasure of watching the Earth leader twitch and die. He was tired of toying with these troublesome monkeys. The Martian leader called a meeting.

During the next few minutes, the atmosphere aboard the ship changed. Nathalie and Donald could feel it, even though they were still just specimens on a shelf.

"Did you feel that? The ship has changed course," Kessler observed.

"I'm scared!" Nathalie whimpered.

"Oh, Nathalie, if only I could hold you in my arms," Donald moaned.

"Oh, Donald!"

Kessler was frustrated. "I simply don't know

what's going on anymore," he said. For a scientist, that was greater torture than any mere pain of the flesh.

What Nathalie and Donald couldn't see was the immense room at the core of the command ship. Rank on rank of fierce Martian warriors lined the galleries and balconies of the mammoth metal arena. Gigantic robots watched over the rally.

And then began an ancient Martian rite. Ferocious Martian warriors had performed this ceremony for countless ages. From the time a Martian hatched and killed its siblings, this ritual was its only goal.

The rite of conquest celebrated the Martians' unquenchable thirst for blood and destruction. There were no more savage creatures in the universe. The Martians thrived on pain and suffering.

They had long since exterminated all rivals and all other life forms on their red planet. They lived a hard, cruel existence beneath the surface, in tunnels and caves carved out by their tremendous technology.

For centuries they had coveted the cool green

Earth with its rich resources and soft, flabby creatures. Now the moment had come for Mars to attack!

The arena floor opened from the center. A globe rose up. On top of the globe stood the Martian leader, splendid in his purple ceremonial robes.

The sphere stopped in midair. A map of the Earth became visible on its surface. The Martian warriors cheered.

Their leader made a stirring speech in their squeaking, clattering tongue. At intervals, the warriors would screech back in unison. Martian flags were raised. Weapons were drawn. The leader made a circle in the air with his arm. The warriors made circles too.

Then the leader reached under his purple cloak and brought forth a flame, burning in the palm of his bony hand. The flame did not harm him. The Earth globe sank to the floor.

The leader touched his flame to the globe. The sphere instantly ignited! The fire harmlessly licked around the leader's robes and legs. Thousands of warriors raised their shrill voices in a mighty Martian battle cry!

Even out in the far rim of the saucer, Nathalie and Donald heard the gruesome cheers. They were afraid. Both knew instinctively that now was the time when Mars would attack.

* ★ * *

Washington, D.C.

Calm heads prevailed in the morning. The White House carried on as if nothing had happened. The public needed to see strength. The Secret Service had been discreetly tripled. Other measures had been quietly taken. But to the average observer, the White House appeared to function as it would on any other day.

A school tour group was beginning to make its way through the historic halls. They were gathered in the Blue Room, just inside the curved colonnade of the north portico.

Among the inner-city students selected for a surprise photo op were Cedric and Neville Williams. The boys were on their best behavior. They were taking this opportunity to improve their minds.

Upstairs in the Oval Office, President James Dale tried to get his mind off what had happened just hours earlier. The bones of his beloved dog, Rusty, were being buried in the Rose Garden, beneath his favorite bush.

Down the hall was the President's bedroom. The once-peaceful sanctuary that had rested so many great heads was scarred with the scorching heat of a Martian ray. Marsha was so upset, she couldn't even think about which pattern to choose for replacing the wallpaper. The President's world was unraveling. Martian saucers filled the skies.

Dispatches came in from all over. In the air over Washington, the Martians shot down a squadron of jets. A Martian saucer had tipped the majestic spire of the Washington Monument.

Dale's head drooped. Just days before, his biggest worry had been reelection. Now he was fighting a war with monsters from outer space!

James Dale wasn't a quitter. He'd been in tough races before. There had to be some way to defeat this Martian menace. Every opponent had a weakness.

The brains had to come up with something.

Government labs had autopsied the Martian assassin. Had they found anything that could be used against the disgusting things?

The President read a faxed lab report. The Martian assassin's blue chewing gum turned out to be pure nitrogen. The gum was a clever means for the creature to breathe Earth's atmosphere. Okay, but how could you use that information to kill them?

"It's a full-scale invasion!" a voice exclaimed.

The President glanced up to see Mitch, the Secret Service agent. Through the row of windows behind the President, Mitch was watching a sky filled with flying saucers. A circular shadow fell on the north lawn of the White House. The agent said, "We need to get you to safety."

The bomb-proof command post in the cellar was out of the question. Mitch and his men intended to get the President to a helicopter waiting on the south lawn.

A saucer dropped onto the north lawn. Martian troops swarmed from the silvery disk.

Dale was hustled into the hall, where he and his family were surrounded by a squad of Secret

Service agents. The agents herded the First Family downstairs.

"Shouldn't we go that way?" Marsha waved her arms toward the nearest exit, in the Blue Room.

"Sorry, ma'am, there's a tour going through," Mitch said in a monotone.

In the Blue Room, James Monroe's portrait exploded as a Martian ray disintegrated a wall of paintings. Kids screamed and ran like rats. Secret Service men rushed to defend the students, only to be cut down by Martian fire.

The White House was burning! Smoke fogged the air. For a moment, Cedric and Neville couldn't even see each other. They were covered in chunks of antique plaster and bits of shredded canvas that minutes ago had been national treasures.

Cedric and Neville crawled out of the rubble. The Secret Service agents lay before them, and so did a pair of pistols.

Cedric earned his A in marksmanship when he put a bullet in the brain of a rampaging Martian.

Somewhere in the smoke between the Green Room and the East Room, James Dale coughed.

"Where's Taffy?" The President and First Lady had become separated from their daughter.

An explosion jangled the ornate red chandelier overhead.

"Keep moving, Mr. President! We have to get you to the back stairs," Mitch said.

A Martian leaped from a doorway. He exchanged fire with Mitch. Then the Martian's ray swept across the ceiling.

The First Lady gasped, "The Nancy Reagan chandelier!" just as the massive gilt light fixture crushed her with a musical crash.

President Dale was in the Martian's sights. PA-PA-POW!

The invader's head exploded. The creature slid to the floor. Mitch stared in amazement at the two teenagers holding smoking pistols.

"What you gawking at! Get the President out of here," Cedric commanded. Then he and his brother swung in a synchronized move to blast another Martian.

Mitch scrambled to his feet. His left arm hung limply at his side. As shock gave way to pain, he realized he had been shot. He grabbed the dazed President and found the door to the stairs.

★ ★ ★

Las Vegas, Nevada

The world was coming to an end. Everyone was talking about it. The headlines read, "MARS TRAGEDY." Millions of people wore Pahrump Massacre T-shirts. There were Martian jokes in Tom Jones's Las Vegas show. Cindy the waitress was getting great tips, like she always did during national disasters.

The world was coming to an end. Barbara Land had seen it. There was no point in trying to be good or live up to oaths. The only twelve steps she was taking were to the bar of the lavish home she shared with Art.

The tycoon didn't even notice how sick his wife was. Barbara tried to tell him. She'd tried to tell everybody. She got Art to stare at the TV. But she could tell he was just pretending to look at the awful images.

Art was like a machine that couldn't stop. It was always the deal, the money, what he wanted, and what he could get. Nothing else mattered to him. And Barbara was invisible. No one could see her. No one listened to her.

Barbara staggered into the living room. Art paced the plush carpet with a phone glued to his ear. He was yapping about limos for every investor and top-of-the-line leather interiors.

"Hello! Martians have attacked!" Barbara screeched. "Are you still worried about that crazy hotel? Don't you realize what's happened?"

"You're worried about yesterday, and I'm worried about tomorrow," Art snapped. "Martians come to Earth, they need a place to stay like anybody else."

Barbara went berserk. Maybe the human race didn't deserve to live. How could such self-centered creatures survive? She realized she was on her own. She had to make preparations. Barbara grabbed a bottle of booze and marched out.

Suddenly, she had Art's full attention. That was the answer! The Galaxy Hotel limos should each be stocked with a bottle of champagne! That was just the way to say "class" to a visitor from any planet. Art made a mental note as he hurried to get to his meeting at the Galaxy.

A short time later, Art was in full frantic pitch.

"Gambling is a leisure activity that will never go out of style. Just look at the last few days. Even in a time of national crisis, people want to play blackjack!"

All of Art's plans had come together perfectly. A beautiful model of the hotel sat in the center of tables heaped with food and drink. There was live music and gorgeous waitresses.

Some of the richest people in the world had come to Art's meeting. He promised them everything. He guaranteed their investments would be returned in five months. But he felt as if he was losing them. They seemed disturbed by noises outside.

A man with a drawl and a Texas hat said, "Mr. Land, I believe we ought to reconvene this meeting at a later time."

"Five more minutes!" Art begged. The investors were looking right past him! He pumped up the charm. "I want you to see our beautiful showroom. It's stupendous! It will attract the biggest stars!"

Art felt like a comedian whose act was bombing. He said desperately, "I tell you, there's no way we can lose!"

How could Art know that a Martian saucer was hovering outside the window? He didn't even see the blinding flash of a Martian ray.

Art never knew what hit him. He was buried under the tons of concrete and steel of the Galaxy Hotel.

★

Panic was just starting to spread among the crowds at the Luxor. Mr. Bava stood halfway up the main staircase. Two Roman soldiers posed behind him. The casino manager tried to calm anxious guests. "Please, everyone. If we just keep calm, we can get through this. The army has survived, and they will have the situation under control very soon."

Because Mr. Bava was busy, Byron slipped away to call Louise. He had to fight frantic guests to get a phone.

Byron told Louise his flight had been canceled. All flights had been canceled. The connection was terrible. Byron could barely make out what Louise was saying. She and Cedric and Neville were safe. But the Martians were everywhere! Byron heard gunshots. Then the line went dead!

He had to get to Washington—but how? The

ex-boxer felt helpless rage. Here he was about to get his life back together, put his family together, and these things came out of the sky to tear it all down. It would take a miracle to reach his wife and kids.

"Byron! Byron! Do you know anyone who can fly a plane?"

Byron turned at the sound of the voice. He saw Barbara Land. She was drunk. And she looked desperate.

"Your husband can fly a plane," Byron said.

Barbara shook her head. "No. He's dead." She was very matter of fact. Then she said earnestly, "I told him this was going to happen. I even loaded the plane with supplies. I want to go to the Tahoe Caves. It's remote. The Martians won't find it."

Byron felt hope stir in his heart. She had a plane. This was his miracle! But all he could say was, "Where's the plane?"

"A private airfield on the other side of the freeway," Barbara said.

"Could it fly to Washington, D.C.?" Byron asked.

"Why? I want to go to Tahoe," Barbara replied.

The showroom wall exploded. Tom Jones sprinted out of the stage door. He ran into Byron. "Martian right behind me!" the singer exclaimed.

Seconds before, he'd been coolly crooning "She's a lady," when Martians came onstage. They mocked his act! Then they started shooting!

Jones didn't have time to tell Byron what had happened. A Martian soldier leaped through the smoking hole in the showroom wall.

Byron's fist slammed into its helmet. Green gas poured out. The Martian shrieked and died, twitching on the floor.

"That was a heck of a punch!" Jones said.

"Get his gun. You might need it," Byron advised. Jones took the larger weapon. Byron removed a ray pistol from the Martian's belt. He didn't want anything to get between him and that plane.

A little group formed around Byron's solid presence. There was Cindy the waitress, a rude gambler, Barbara, and Tom Jones. They heard explosions and screaming in the streets outside.

"We've got to get out of here!" Jones exclaimed.

"You know how to fly a plane?" Byron asked.

"You got one?" the singer countered.

"She does." Byron pointed at Barbara. She regretted her lapse into alcohol. She'd lost faith. And here was a pilot and some brave people. There was hope yet!

Byron also felt grateful. It's not every day that you're saved from Martians by a celebrity who can fly.

But first they had to reach the plane. The little party crept outside the casino. Cars were overturned and burning. Byron was frightened. The streets of Las Vegas were dark, lit only by raging fires and the flash of Martian armament. People ran shrieking down the street, pursued by flying Martians.

The airborne aliens carried a speaker that croaked robotic promises of friendship. "Have a nice day. We come in peace. Don't run. We are your friends." The promises mingled with the hiss of their hideous weapons. Tourists dropped in droves.

Byron's little band dodged from car to truck to burning bus as they made their way across the freeway. A Martian popped from behind a wrecked tour bus. Tom Jones dropped him with a single shot. Barbara and Cindy took the cremated creature's weapons.

A jeep overloaded with soldiers careened past. A Martian warrior with a jet pack swooped down like a bird of prey. His ravaging ray ripped into the jeep's driver.

The boxy little vehicle swerved and rolled and flipped into a gun emplacement. A flying saucer glided over a building and blasted more rays into the army's defensive works.

Thus occupied, the Martians ignored Byron and his fellow fugitives. They came to a graveyard of old casino signs: a massive silver slipper, a giant Aladdin's lamp encrusted with lightbulbs, and half a Titan cowboy. Byron ripped open the wire fencing.

"What are you doing?" Barbara asked. "The airport's this way."

"Shortcut," Byron replied. "The airstrip is on the other side of this complex. Fewer Martians if we go this way."

"How do you know?" the rude gambler challenged. "Just because you're dressed like Caesar doesn't mean you're a leader."

Byron ignored him and squeezed through the

fence. Everyone else followed. The sky was full of tracer fire. Distant army artillery desperately tried to shoot down flying saucers.

As they tiptoed through the relics of old Las Vegas, Byron said quietly, "Tom, after we get to Tahoe, I want you to fly me to Washington, D.C. My wife and kids are there."

Tom looked sad. "I'm sorry. Even if we could make it, Washington must be a war zone. It would be suicide."

"Then show me how to fly the plane," Byron said grimly. "I'll go on my own."

"He's lost! He's led us into a maze!" the gambler griped. He looked around at a giant fish and a bucking bronco the size of a barn.

The gambler had no idea where he was. These meatheads didn't know what they were doing. He was going back to the hotel.

He didn't get ten feet before he ran smack into a Martian! Its scary red eyes looked at him like he was a bug.

"Look, I surrender, okay?" said the man. "You understand what that means? You're intelligent beings. Let's cut a deal. I can help you. I'm a lawyer. You want to conquer the world, you'll need lawyers." The gambler thought he was getting through to the gruesome guy. He held out his watch. "Hey, you want my Rolex?"

Then the man's skull plopped to the ground with the rest of his bones. But the Martian who killed him was also dead.

Barbara's ray gun was still smoking. Tom Jones complimented her on the shot. But Barbara was staring past the gory scene. "Look!" she said. "The airfield!" A crushed, burning plane flickered on the pocked runway.

Barbara felt frightened, but full of hope. "That's where the plane is, right there in that hangar."

★ ★ ★

Washington, D.C.

"What happened to Marsha? Is she dead? And where's Taffy?" the President moaned. He slumped over the big round table at the head of the Pentagon's war room.

The heavily fortified, massively defended war room was designed to resist nuclear attack. The generals hoped the President was safe. But the Martian weapons made them more than a little nervous.

Video displays glowed and blipped. Blinking green lights showed the unstoppable progress of the Martian forces. The alien attack was worldwide and devastating.

James Dale was in over his head. He didn't care that the French president was on the phone. He didn't care about any of this crazy nightmare. Dale mumbled, "Where did I go wrong? I should have stayed in local politics. I was happier back then."

"It's important." A military aide pressed a phone into Dale's shaking hand.

The President slurred, "Hello," followed by an indifferent *"Comment ca vas?"*

The president of France was jubilant. He had negotiated an agreement with the Martians.

Dale screamed, "Get out! Get out now!"

Then he heard the sickening sound of Martian weapons. He pictured the French capital blazing like a bonfire, and the Eiffel Tower toppled by marauding Martians. The crafty creatures had tricked every world leader.

General Decker hovered like a specter of death. "Mr. President, I need you to sign this." He pressed a pen into Dale's limp fingers.

"What is it? My last will and testament?" Dale wondered.

"No, sir! It's your order to deploy our nuclear capability," Decker said crisply.

Dale had no choice. He signed the papers.

General Decker was deeply satisfied. The President had finally done the right thing. Orders were barked. Buttons were pushed. With clockwork precision, the most awesome fighting force on Earth was unleashed upon the evil hordes.

A silvery missile streaked from its silo. General Decker stared at the war-room monitor. He was proud to see the rocket's red glare carry the fight into the enemy's orbiting base. He watched the starry skies, eager to see the deadly bloom of the nuclear mushroom.

Secret satellites gave vivid closeups of the Martian mother ship. The missile was within range of its target when a hatch opened on the ship. A small balloon floated out of the open hatch. The odd object sported little antennae and a nozzle, like a toy trumpet.

The American missile detonated—a fierce flash in the blackness of space. Decker expected to see the disk reduced to debris.

Instead, the nozzle on the little balloon sucked up the explosion. Then it floated back into the mother ship.

"What happened?" Decker squeaked. His highest hopes had been deflated.

The screen blacked out. It was replaced by a transmission from the Martian mother ship. A high-ranking Martian held the little balloon. He put the nozzle in his lipless mouth and breathed deeply.

The Martian spoke in a high, squeaky voice. Then he cracked up laughing. Other Martians were laughing too, like frat boys at a party. The interplanetary bullies gloated. Earth's worst weapon was a party favor for them!

Once again, the screen went blank. The war room was silent, but for the hiss of static. No one moved to turn off the monitors. The room felt like a funeral parlor. The President's face was pale. His eyes were far away.

Mitch's wounded arm throbbed. He whispered under his breath, "Only God can help us now."

But incoming dispatches proved that nothing stopped the Martians. While explosions rocked Washington, the President and his staff read reports. From time to time the lights blinked.

The Martians waged an insane campaign. They followed no known military strategy. What drove these skull-faced thugs? There seemed to be no purpose to their malice. They appeared to delight in tricking and torturing unsuspecting beings. They killed everything that moved.

Their weapons were unbeatable, though they looked like the demented doodlings of a crazed comic-book artist or the wild designs of a sci-fi thriller. The President had never enjoyed such entertainments because they never seemed real. But here he sat in the war room with the planet in ruins.

Martians murdered millions in Manhattan! The streets of New York were piled with bones.

In London, the flying fiends bashed Big Ben to smithereens! They used Egypt's pyramids as croquet wickets. The Martians spray-painted the Taj Mahal.

The devilish destroyers used fantastic machines to go bowling with boulders on Easter Island. Giant robots kicked cars through the St.

Louis Arch. The lunatic destruction made it seem as if Earth had been invaded by cartoon cats and ducks who dropped atomic anvils and gave electronic hot feet.

No earthly monument was safe. Human history meant nothing to them. The planet was their playground—and these were not nice kids!

Then came the most horrible indignity of all: Martian saucers used their deadly rays to recarve Mt. Rushmore into hideous alien faces!

The lights went out and were slow in coming back on. Decker paced the war room, pistol poised. "Quiet! I can hear something," the general hissed. He tensed, ready for battle.

Everyone heard tiny footsteps patter down the hall outside the bunker door. Then the room rocked! Concrete and steel whizzed in on a cloud of smoke. Glass broke. Things fell. And when the dust settled, a huge hole had replaced the door.

A blinking green orb rolled through the hole. It stopped in the middle of the room. Its flashing light reflected everywhere. It thrummed like a living thing. The surviving staff members dived for cover behind tables and chairs. Every eye was on the puzzling, pulsing orb.

The Martian leader and six officers marched briskly into the war room. The officers leveled weapons in a protective circle. The leader picked up the mysterious green orb and shook it. The humans in the room could clearly see it was a Martian snow-globe toy.

The Martians laughed, a mirthless, mocking sound.

Decker's face flushed red as he stood, a pistol in each hand. "You think you can come over here and do whatever you want?" he roared. "Well, you don't know human beings!"

Decker emptied both pistols into the Martian squad. The bullets pinged harmlessly off their space armor and ricocheted around the room. The general bellowed, "We'll never surrender!"

The Martian leader gave an order. Three officers seized Decker. He was disarmed and pushed against the wall, still protesting that he would never give up.

The Martian leader produced a tiny, toylike gun, the size of a cereal prize. His officers leaped clear of Decker. The tiny gun discharged a bizarre blast of energy.

In seconds, General Decker was shrunk to

three inches tall! Still, the military mite squeaked defiant oaths. He shook his little fists and charged the leader.

The Martian watched with amusement, then raised its boot and squashed Decker like a bug.

The humans ran for the exit! Martian weapons fizzed and whined. Bones clattered on the carpet. Mitch jumped in front of a gun and saved his nation's leader one last time.

President Dale looked up from Mitch's mortal remains. He stared straight into the malignant, scarlet eyes of the leader.

James Dale spoke from his heart. "Why are you doing this? Isn't the universe big enough for both of us? What is wrong with you people? Why be enemies just because we're different? There's nothing we couldn't accomplish with Earth and Mars working together. Why destroy, when you can create? We can have it all, or we can smash it all. Which is better? Why can't we just get along?"

The Martians listened to James Dale's last speech. They seemed impressed. The leader offered his hand. Dale was surprised, but he reached out to take it. Maybe he had salvaged the situation after all. Maybe they could see reason.

Then the Martian's hand came off! It crawled up the President's sleeve. Its shiny fingers crept like spider's legs up the front of his Cerutti suit. The fake hand had a tiny tail where the wrist would be.

Dale barely had time to stammer "What is that?" before the hand had scurried over his shoulder. Then its tail uncurled and jabbed into the President's back.

The sharp point of the spike pushed through his chest. James Dale, President of the United States of America, fell dead on his back on a map of the world. The gleaming spike grew and sprouted a Martian flag.

All was quiet. The Martians had won.

★ ★ ★ ★

Perkinsville

In a matter of days, the Norris trailer had become a shrine to Billy-Glenn. The family had every piece of Billy-Glenn merchandise, including a bronze bust.

Richie had never seen his dad and mom so upset. They lightened up a little bit when Congress was fried. But even the utter destruction of the hated tax-takers did not bring them out of their funk.

It was a relief to get to the donut shop. At least he didn't have to see much of Billy-Glenn. Richie loved his brother and all, but this hero dude they kept talking about on the TV wasn't much like the Billy-Glenn he remembered.

Richie had been on a donut break when the Senate was barbecued. He was puzzled by the Martians' behavior. "What did they do that for?" he had asked Rosie.

"Maybe they don't like the Earth people," the waitress had said dully. Aliens had landed, and Rosie was still bored. Well, she didn't stay bored for long.

A flying saucer set down right beside the donut shop. A ray sliced through the building, like a hot knife through butter. Richie didn't see what happened to Rosie. He ran!

Richie was way out of breath when he reached the Norris family trailer. He'd seen Martian soldiers zapping people just down the road.

Dogs were barking. Stuff was blowing up.

Richie told his parents about the saucer by the donut shop. He figured the family belonged together at a time like this. "Give me the keys to the truck. I'm gonna get Grandma." Richie held out his hand.

Glenn slapped a .45 in the outstretched palm. "You forget Grandma. She's halfway to outer space already. The shells are in that box on the table."

Sue-Ann snapped a shotgun shut. "I tell you one thing. They ain't getting the TV."

Richie grabbed the truck keys off the Formica table.

"Where are you going?" Glenn demanded.

"I'm going to get Grandma," Richie said.

"You ain't goin' nowhere!" Glenn asserted. "You're going to stay here and defend this trailer."

"That's what Billy-Glenn would do," Sue-Ann chimed in.

Richie was stunned. This was Grandma!

"You leave here, you're disgracing an American hero," Dad shouted. He pointed at all the Billy-Glenn junk stuffing the trailer.

"I don't care. I'm gonna get Grandma." Richie squeezed past his dad and slipped out the door.

As the screen slammed, he heard Mom yell, "Richie, come back!"

There was this weird humming in the sky. Richie's hands were shaking so much he could barely get the keys in the ignition. A Martian saucer hovered over the trailer park.

Richie gunned the engine, and the truck roared down the road. He looked in his rearview mirror. Out of the saucer came huge, pincerlike hands. The hands reached down, grabbed the Norris trailer and another trailer, then smashed them together, crushing them like aluminum cans.

Richie couldn't look in the mirror anymore. His parents were gone. He put the pedal to the metal. He had to get to Grandma!

And it wasn't easy. Richie saw totally insane stuff. These Martians were out of their giant brains! Their weapons were like big toys or nightmares out of old monster movies.

Richie wasn't far from the home when he glanced back and saw that the truck was being chased by this gnarly robot! He could see a little

Martian dude in the glass dome of the robot's head. It grinned that wicked Martian grin.

Richie was desperate! He looked around for any kind of chance. He spotted the power-line pylons like skeletons standing in a row over the hills.

The idea was crazy, but it just might work. Richie yanked the steering wheel and swerved off the road. The truck bounced over a rough field. His arms felt like they were going to shake out of his shoulders. Richie risked a glance in the rearview. The robot was running behind him.

Then the big metal dude made a big metal mistake. The mistake Richie wanted him to make. The robot collided with a power pylon. High-tension lines broke and snapped like angry anacondas spitting sparks.

Richie swerved to avoid the cascade of electricity. The robot shuddered and danced in a rock 'em, sock 'em rhythm. Thousands of volts scorched it to a shell.

Richie was back on the highway, speeding to the rescue. He felt like he was in the kind of nightmare where you run and run and never get anywhere.

But then he saw the driveway to Grandma's home. The Lawrence Welk Retirement Village was just beyond the power pylons. Richie was worried. The giant robot might already have stomped Grandma! At the very least, it meant there were Martians in the area.

Richie drove the truck straight up the wide front steps of the home. Right away he could see things were bad. Scorched skeletons lay on the lawn. The doors were broken down.

Richie grabbed the .45, crouched low, and ran into the unknown. He picked his way past toasted wheelchairs and melted walkers littering the lobby. Nasty smoke curled off fried vinyl chairs. Richie coughed.

He crept down the dark hall to Grandma's room. Just inside he saw three green, grinning Martians pointing a huge ray gun at Grandma!

The sweet old lady was knitting a shawl and listening to her favorite record. With the earphones on, she was unaware of the disaster that had befallen those around her.

Richie saw the Martians just as the Martians saw him. He ducked a fraction of a second before a Martian ray obliterated the top of the door. The wood exploded with a *whoosh!*

Grandma jerked her head at the sound. That short, sharp movement tugged the headphone plug out of its socket. The stereo switched from *private* to *speaker.*

Suddenly, the room was filled with the sound of Slim Whitman in full-throated yokel yodel! Richie winced at the noise blasting from the speakers.

The Martians looked queasy. Their nasty red eyes bulged. Many green capillaries burst in their big brains, which pulsed rapidly. The Martians squealed.

As each Martian's brain exploded, Grandma exclaimed, "Oh, Richie! I'm awful worried. Look at these men here. I think they're sick."

"What's killing 'em?" Richie wondered.

"My music." Grandma smiled.

Richie was amazed. "What music?"

Then he realized the horrible noise was some kind of singing. This was Grandma's favorite album? Whoa, it takes all kinds.

But this was the perfect music for the occasion. With a wall of sound blasting from the speakers, they were safe. So Richie spent a little time with some big speakers and batteries hooking up an awesome stereo system to the truck.

For a moment, he thought, *Dad's gonna kill me.* Then he realized Dad was gone. Richie was the head of the household now. And Richie was going to make sure Grandma was all right.

They cruised, and Richie had an idea. If this music killed the Martians in the Retirement Village, maybe it would work everywhere else. It was like audio bug spray for the biggest, baddest bugs that ever crashed Earth's picnic.

Richie and Grandma motored through town. Everywhere they looked, Martians looted stores and homes. They stole stuff just to smash it.

Then they heard Slim's voice. Brains popped, and Martians dropped in their tracks! It worked!

On the horizon, Richie saw exactly what he was looking for: the radio station.

Las Vegas, Nevada

Cannon rumbled like summer thunder in the distance. Little flashes popped on the dark horizon. Byron and his comrades scurried across the open space of the runway. They made it to the safety of the darkened hangar.

Barbara's twin-engine Cessna spread its white wings in the gloom behind the sliding door. The mammoth building was silent as a cemetery. Byron and Cindy stayed behind to open the huge hangar doors. Tom and Barbara climbed into the Cessna's cockpit.

Barbara rearranged supplies to make room for the extra passengers. Tom started his preflight checklist. He flipped switches on the instrument panel. "I can fly this," he muttered. Then he accidentally turned on the radio. Outrageous yodeling split the silence.

Byron and Cindy jumped. Barbara bumped her head at the startling sound. Jones flicked off the radio, his ears ringing with Slim's vocals. "Who put that on the radio?" the singer wondered.

The hangar doors were stuck. Byron tugged with all his might until he felt the latch give.

The Cessna's engines coughed and clattered, then hummed.

Just as the hangar doors began to open, Byron and Cindy saw a squad of Martians on the runway! Cindy froze in fear.

Byron whispered, "They haven't seen us. Quick! Get the doors open!"

The waitress and the boxer finished opening the hangar. The plane taxied forward. Tom Jones cried, "That's the Martian Ambassador!"

Byron also recognized the Ambassador. That monster was the incarnation of evil! Louise and his sons might be dead because of that thing. Countless others already were. Countless more would die unless someone stopped him!

And there was no way the plane was going to take off without the Martians seeing it. Byron knew what he had to do.

"Cindy, you go," Byron said. "I'll draw them off." He knew in his heart that God gave him permission to release the bull.

"What?" Cindy was overloaded with shock.

Byron pushed her toward the plane. She ran.

Byron loped out of the hangar. He was headed for the Martians.

"He's flipped!" Tom Jones said. "We can't leave him."

Cindy closed the plane's hatch behind her. "He's letting us get away." Her voice choked with emotion. "It's what he said." And it was what she had seen in his eyes.

Jones revved the plane's engines.

"Hi, guys! How are you doing?" Byron asked almost casually.

The Martians turned to face him. Byron dropped his weapon and raised his arms so they could see he was unarmed. He held up his fists. "Come on!" he called. "Come on, you cowards!"

The Martian Ambassador broke away from the squad. He understood the universal call to a duel. And he was sure he would win against a puny Earthling. He stalked up to Byron and dropped his own weapon.

Byron smacked his famous left against the Ambassador's helmet. The Ambassador punched back. Byron dodged and weaved. He felt light on his feet, like back in his training days. He skipped around like a kid.

Byron planted another hard left hook to the Martian's helmet. The Ambassador was a bit dazed, but he put up his own fists, ready to continue the match. Byron danced away from the hangar. The Ambassador eagerly followed. At least this Earthling knew the pleasure of a good fight! The Ambassador would enjoy killing this one.

The other Martians were also excited. They chattered and gleeped in their squeaky language. They formed a ring around the fighters. They were so focused on the fight that they failed to see the Cessna creep out of the hangar.

Byron saw the plane out of the corner of his eye. And when it reached the open runway, Byron used his best Sunday punch to shatter the Ambassador's helmet. Green gas puffed out. The Martian screeched and fell dying at Byron's feet.

Three Martians rushed the boxer. His flying fists greeted them. Four more joined in, then another five. Oddly, Byron was happy. For the first time in years, he had a good, clean fight to sink his fists into.

But the Martians kept pouring in. The squad swarmed over Byron like ants on a carcass.

The Cessna's wheels left the earth. The plane rose and banked steeply around. Jones, Barbara, and Cindy saw the mass of Martians move away from the boxer's body. They weren't looking at the broken remains of Byron Williams. They were looking at the all-time champ of the world!

★ ★ ★ ★

Washington, D.C.

"Something's happened to Byron," Louise Williams said to her sons. For a moment, despite the noise and terror around them, she had sensed her husband's spirit.

Then, above the roar of weapons and fire, Louise heard a strange howling sound. Was it music? Was it some new Martian torture?

If Louise could have seen outside her barricaded apartment, she would have known military helicopters with speakers circled the city. The musical stylings of Slim Whitman radiated over the nation's capital.

Martian soldiers fell like flies. Saucers wobbled and crashed. The military wasn't alone in fighting the fiendish invaders. Tuned to the right station, a boom box was better than a bazooka! Many Martians fell.

The song had passed from Perkinsville to Wichita, and from there all around the world. Slim's voice killed platoons of Martians from London to Timbuktu.

Missiles and bullets and bombs had been completely useless. Now the military flew jets playing music! A squadron of the jets pursued the Martian command ship.

Nathalie and Donald saw the Martian leader and his lackeys clutch their throbbing craniums and fall to the deck. Out of control, the saucer tilted. All the specimens in the lab slid off shelves and smashed on the floor. The Martians writhed and squealed.

Donald's head sloshed among broken glass and his splattered organs on the deck. Nathalie's head became detached from the Chihuahua's body and rolled up next to Donald's.

"Good-bye, darling. I wish things could have been different," he whispered.

Nathalie fluttered her eyes. "So do I."

The romantic moment was spoiled when the Martian leader's head exploded like a ripe melon.

The lovers were splattered with green goop.

Nathalie felt herself losing power. She said, "Good-bye. I love you."

Donald said, "I love you too, Nathalie."

With her last breath, Nathalie kissed him on the lips. Just as her eyes shut, Nathalie thought, "I can't be over. There are always reruns." Then she faded to black.

Careening out of control, the Martian mother ship crashed into the Atlantic Ocean. The remaining fleet of forty flying saucers fled the Earth's atmosphere and sought safety in the silence of space.

★ ★ ★

Earth

At dawn, a robin sang on a branch, just as the sun peeped over the mountains at Lake Tahoe. Barbara, Cindy, and Tom Jones came out of the cave, blinking in the fresh light of a new day. It was more than a new day. It was the beginning of a new era for humankind.

All across America, people cleaned up. They repaired windows, tore down dangerous ruins, cleared roads, and swept the streets. They tended the wounded and buried the dead. Debris and garbage were burned.

All of this was performed without words. No one spoke the whole day. There was no traffic, no video or radio. The silence was extraordinary.

At dusk, a small party gathered on the steps of the shattered Capitol building. The glare of TV lights interrupted the sunset. The cameras were held by students.

A small crowd of survivors stood as witnesses to this event. These were tough, clever people. Lucky people.

Cedric and Neville, with pistols in their belts, stood side by side with their mother. Their faces were grim. They'd gotten the word about Byron. Everyone knew about the Champ.

On the steps stood six Marines in crumpled, dirty uniforms. They were the honor guard for the living national heroes, Richie and Grandma Norris.

Taffy Dale had survived the attack on the White House. She approached the Perkinsville natives. Taffy was flanked by two elderly letter carriers. The three of them were all that remained of the United States government.

Taffy cleared her throat. "Florence Norris, I am proud to present you with the Congressional Medal of Honor, the highest decoration our nation can bestow."

She hung the medal around Grandma's scrawny neck and kissed both soft, wrinkled cheeks. Taffy hoped she did it right.

Grandma said, "Thank you, dear."

Then Taffy faced Richie. She was the most beautiful girl he had ever seen up close! She was even more beautiful when she blushed under his gaze.

But Taffy got her cool back. She said, "Richard Norris, on behalf of my parents, who couldn't be here today, for saving the world from the Martians, I hereby award you the Medal of Honor."

She put the medal around Richie's neck, and felt suddenly shy. He was so cute!

"You don't have to kiss me if you don't want to," Richie said humbly, which made him even cuter.

Taffy looked a little exasperated. "I've got to." So she kissed him quickly on both cheeks.

They were both still blushing when Richie said, "I, uh, prepared a speech. Is that okay?"

"Sure. I think that's very appropriate," Taffy said.

Richie took a crumpled piece of paper from his pocket. He bit his lip and mumbled a little. Then he seized a shred of confidence and said, "Well, folks, I just want to say I didn't really . . . I mean, there's lots of people in the world who did more than I have. And they should be here now getting a medal too. So, uh, we made it, but we almost didn't. It was close. And . . ."

What came next? Oh, duh! Look at the speech.

Richie found his place and continued. "Now we must rebuild. We must rebuild our cities, but maybe not the way they were before. Maybe instead of houses we should live in tepees. It's better in lots of ways."

Richie could tell the crowd liked what he was saying, even if they didn't quite understand it. Richie wasn't even sure he did. But there hadn't been much time for speech writing.

Taffy's eyes were shining in that goofy, girl-likes-you way. Richie warmed to his subject. "And the environment, let's take care of it this time. And let's have a decent justice system that's fair. Then we won't need so many lawyers and psychiatrists. Do they really help? If we get society right this time, we don't need 'em!"

The crowd applauded.

"And there's no need to cut military or government spending now, because that's been, like, taken care of."

The crowd cheered.

"The future's gonna be great! Let's go for it!" Richie shouted. He looked around. "I guess that's all I have to say. Thank you."

He stepped away from the cameras. The crowd still clapped and cheered. But now that it was over, Richie felt nervous. Had he just made a jerk of himself? He asked Taffy, "Was that all right?"

She said, "Yeah." Then she smiled. "Have you got a girlfriend?"

The first citizens of the new Earth looked up into the starry sky. They weren't afraid of anything. They would be ready the next time Mars attacked!